Step into Science

What Just Happened?

Reading Results and Making Inferences

Paul Challen

Science education consultant: Suzy Gazlay

Crabtree Publishing Company

www.crabtreebooks.com

Crabtree Publishing Company

www.crabtreebooks.com

Author: Paul Challen
Series editor: Vashti Gwynn
Editorial director: Paul Humphrey
Editor: Adrianna Morganelli
Proofreader: Reagan Miller
Production coordinator: Katherine Berti
Prepress technician: Katherine Berti
Project manager: Kathy Middleton
Illustration: Stefan Chabluk and Stuart Harrison
Photography: Chris Fairclough
Design: sprout.uk.com
Photo research: Vashti Gwynn

Produced for Crabtree Publishing Company by Discovery Books.

Thanks to models Ottilie and Sorcha Austin-Baker, Dan Brice-Bateman, Matthew Morris, and Amrit and Tara Shoker.

Photographs:
Corbis: JLP/Jose Pelaez: p. 6, 27; Bettmann: p. 21 (right)
Discovery Photo Library: Paul Humphrey: p. 19
Getty Images: Michael Rosenfeld: p. 4 (bottom left);
    Bennett Barthelemy: p. 17 (left); Ryan McVay: p. 20 (left)
Istockphoto: ArtisticCaptures: p. 15 (bottom)
Library of Congress: Edward Lynch: p. 25 (bottom right)
Samara Parent: back cover, p. 1 (top)
Shutterstock: cover, p. 1 (center left and center right), 3,
    9 (bottom), 16 (center top), 29 (center top); Monkey
    Business Images: p. 8; Andreas Gradin: p. 9 (top);
    Michael Onisforou: p. 12; Ami Beyer: p. 14 (left);
    John R. Smith: p. 16 (top right); Micha Rosenwirth:
    p. 22; Sklep Spozywczy: p. 23; Pakhnyushcha: p. 24 (left);
    Kushch Dmitry: p. 26 (right); Elena Elisseeva: p. 28

Library and Archives Canada Cataloguing in Publication

Challen, Paul, 1967-
    What just happened? Reading results and making inferences /
Paul Challen.

(Step into science)
Includes index.
ISBN 978-0-7787-5156-4 (bound).--ISBN 978-0-7787-5171-7 (pbk.)

        1. Science--Methodology--Juvenile literature. 2. Science--
Experiments--Juvenile literature. I. Title. II. Series: Step into science
(St. Catharines, Ont.)

Q175.2.C43 2010   j507.8   C2009-906643-2

Library of Congress Cataloging-in-Publication Data

Challen, Paul C. (Paul Clarence), 1967-
  What just happened? Reading results and making inferences /
Paul Challen.
    p. cm. -- (Step into science)
  Includes index.
  ISBN 978-0-7787-5156-4 (reinforced lib. bdg. : alk. paper)
  -- ISBN 978-0-7787-5171-7 (pbk. : alk. paper)
  1. Science--Methodology--Juvenile literature. I. Title. II. Series.

  Q175.2.C4269 2010
  507.8--dc22

                                                    2009045511

Crabtree Publishing Company

Printed in the U.S.A./122009/CG20091120

www.crabtreebooks.com   1-800-387-7650

Published in Canada
Crabtree Publishing
616 Welland Ave.
St. Catharines, Ontario
L2M 5V6

Published in the United States
Crabtree Publishing
PMB 59051
350 Fifth Avenue, 59th Floor
New York, New York 10118

Published in the United Kingdom
Crabtree Publishing
Maritime House
Basin Road North, Hove
BN41 1WR

Published in Australia
Crabtree Publishing
386 Mt. Alexander Rd.
Ascot Vale (Melbourne)
VIC 3032

CONTENTS

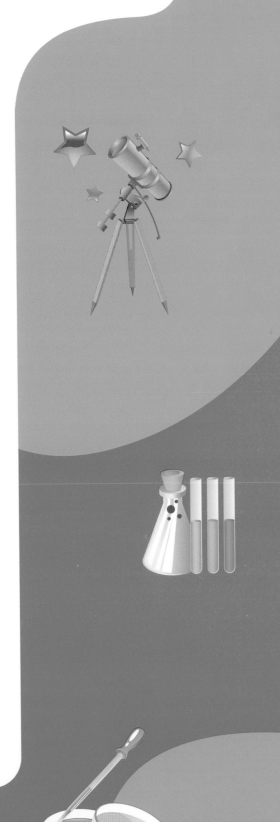

THE SCIENTIFIC METHOD

Have you ever been in an elevator? The **scientific method** is like an elevator—you enter at the first floor and take the elevator up. The elevator passes one floor at a time, and you get closer and closer to your final stop. Sometimes, however, the journey takes you back down before you continue on to reach your destination.

In the same way, following each step in the scientific method is important for making scientific discoveries. Sometimes, though, scientists have to stop, go back, and think again before they continue.

At this point in the scientific method, you can organize the data you have gathered in your experiment. You can do this with graphs, charts, and diagrams. These tools will help you think about the information you have gathered, and about what it means.

◀ This man is experimenting with the design of a new car. He must make sure he organizes his data correctly to get the best design.

Beginning Your Scientific Investigation

Be curious! Questions can come from anywhere, anytime. Questions help scientists make **observations** and do **research**. Science is all about problem-solving!

Making Your Hypothesis

So, what is next? You have a question, and you have done some research. You think you know what will happen when you perform your experiment. The term *hypothesis* means educated guess. So, make a guess and get started!

Designing Your Experiment

How are you going to test your hypothesis? Designing a safe, accurate experiment will give **results** that answer your question.

Collecting and Recording Your Data

During an experiment, scientists make careful observations and record exactly what happens.

Displaying and Understanding Results

Now your **data** can be organized into **graphs, charts,** and **diagrams**. These help you read the information, think about it, and figure out what it means.

Making Conclusions and Answering the Question

So, what did you learn during your experiment? Did your data prove your hypothesis? Scientists share their results so other scientists can try the experiment, or use the results to design another experiment.

GETTING ORGANIZED

Now that you have collected all your data it's time to organize it. One of the best ways to do this is to put it into a **table,** or chart.

A table is a set of rows and columns onto which you record your data. Let's imagine that you've done an experiment with two potted plants.

You water one of the plants every day with plain tap water. The second plant you also water every day with tap water, but add a little plant food once a week.

▼ You should measure your plants carefully each week and record the results.

You make a table in your **journal**, ready for your data. Now, you measure the plants once a week to see how they have grown. You record all the results in your journal for eight weeks.

Your table might look like this:

The table is a useful way of recording your data, but you can get a better picture of what is happening by drawing a graph.

It's important to put all of your data on the table!

| Week | Plant 1 (non-fertilized) | | Plant 2 (fertilized) | |
	height in inches	height in cm	height in inches	height in cm
Week 1	2	5	2	5
Week 2	3	7.75	3.5	8.75
Week 3	4	10.25	5	12.75
Week 4	5	12.75	6.5	16.5
Week 5	5.75	14.5	8	20.25
Week 6	6.5	16.5	9	22.75
Week 7	7	17.75	10	25.5
Week 8	7.5	19	11	28

It's All in the Data

The word "data" comes from the Latin word meaning "something given." In other words, data is something an experiment "gives" you...so don't forget to say thanks!

WHAT IS A GRAPH?

A graph is an easy-to-understand information picture. It is organized to show you the results of an experiment. Graphs use exact measurements to show data. They help scientists to spot patterns in the results of an experiment as well. If something is getting hotter or colder, bigger or smaller, or higher or lower, a graph will show these **trends**.

For example, you can use a graph to show the data from your plant experiment on pages 6-7. You can create a **bar graph** to show this data. The bar graph will show the height of each plant at times that you took your measurements.

▼ You could draw a graph to show the different heights of the children in your class.

The graph will show how the plants grow, week after week. You will see a pattern developing as the plants grow taller.

▲ You could draw a graph to show how fast your heart beats when you are resting and when you are exercising.

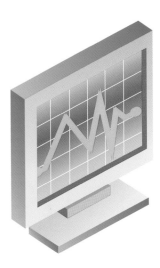

"That's Weird"

Look for bits of odd or unusual information that might creep into your graph. These are called **anomalies**. For example, let's think about your plant experiment. Perhaps your graph shows that one of the plants grew in a gradual pattern. Then, all of a sudden the plant grew a huge amount in one week! Is this possible? It might be, but it is more likely that you made some mistake in measurement. Or, perhaps you forgot to measure the plant one week. Graphs help you to spot anomalies. Then, you can go back to the notes you made during your experiment. These might help you see where you might have gone wrong.

A BAR GRAPH

So how do you use a graph to organize the data you recorded in your scientific experiment? It's actually quite easy!

Take a look at the table from our plant experiment.

Week	Plant 1 (non-fertilized) height in inches	Plant 1 (non-fertilized) height in cm	Plant 2 (fertilized) height in inches	Plant 2 (fertilized) height in cm
Week 1	2	5	2	5
Week 2	3	7.75	3.5	8.75
Week 3	4	10.25	5	12.75
Week 4	5	12.75	6.5	16.5
Week 5	5.75	14.5	8	20.25
Week 6	6.5	16.5	9	22.75
Week 7	7	17.75	10	25.5
Week 8	7.5	19	11	28

On graph paper, you draw a **vertical** (upright) line on the left hand side, and a **horizontal** (across) line along the bottom. Mark the heights in inches up the vertical line, and the number of weeks along the horizontal line. Like this:

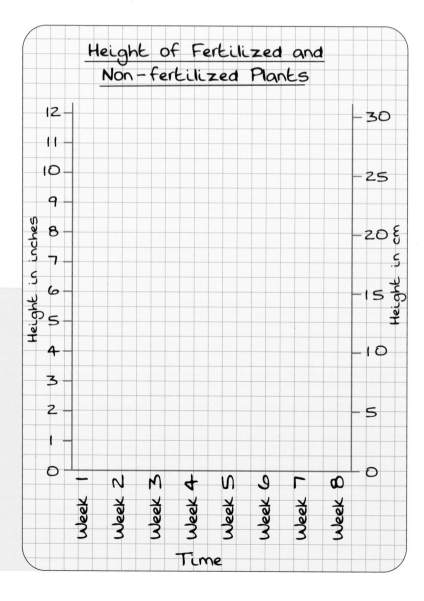

Imperial or Metric?

Imperial and **metric** measurements are two different ways of measuring things. On the graphs and tables in this book, we have shown both. However, you should only use one or the other in your own graphs and tables. Remember to label your measurements clearly!

To begin, use your measurements from week one to draw a bar showing each plant's height for that week. Both bars go up to the two inches (five cm) point. You must use different colors to show the bars for each plant.

By week two plant 1 is three inches (7.75 cm) high. Find the place on the horizontal side where it reads "Week 2." From here you draw a bar up to the three inches (7.75 cm) mark.

Plant 2 has grown to three and a half inches (8.75 cm), so you draw a bar up to the three and a half inches (8.75 cm) mark. Now add bars for all the other weeks, too.

Don't forget to give your graph a title and a color key. Then, you will remember which bar refers to which plant.

Your bar graph will look like this:

Raise the bar! Create a graph!

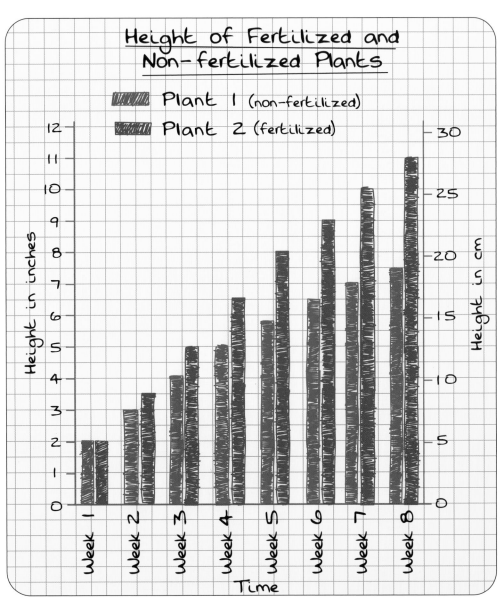

LET'S EXPERIMENT!

Favorite Foods

Problem

You want to take your friends out for your birthday party. But you want to go to the right place to eat. What are your friends' favorite foods? First, you must make a hypothesis.

1 Make a **tally chart** in your journal or on your paper. It should have two columns and about eight rows. Put the headings "Type of Meal" and "Number" in the top row. In the left-hand column write down a list of different meals, like "Hamburger and Fries," or "Spaghetti Bolognese." Mark the bottom row "Other." In the right-hand column you can keep a tally.

Materials:

- ☑ a journal or some paper
- ☑ a ruler
- ☑ a pencil
- ☑ graph paper
- ☑ several friends

► Maybe pizza will be the favorite food among your friends.

2 Talk to as many friends as you can. You probably need at least 10-12 people. Ask them one at a time which of the meals they like best. In the right-hand column make a tally showing the food they choose. If they don't like any of the choices or prefer something else, put a tally next to "Other."

▼ Make sure you complete your tally chart carefully.

3 One of your friends might say a food that has already been said. In this case, put another tally next to that food in the right-hand column.

4 When you have asked all your friends, add up how many tallies each food has.

5 Which food is the most popular? Which is the least?

6 Now make a bar graph on graph paper. It should list the meals along the bottom of the graph. The number of friends that choose each meal will go up the side of the graph.

Type of Meal	Number
Hamburger and Fries	III
Spaghetti Bolognese	I
Baked Potato	IIII
Pizza	I
Curry	II
Tacos	III
Other	I

OTHER KINDS OF DRAWINGS

As well as bar graphs, there are other important kinds of drawings that are very helpful in showing the results of an experiment. Two of these are line plots and pictograms.

To make a line plot you mark Xs or other symbols in lines to show numbers of something. For example, let's say you were drawing a line plot showing the eye colors of your friends. Three of your friends have blue eyes. Five have green eyes and four have brown eyes. Your line plot will look like this:

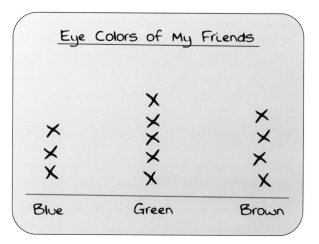

Eye Colors of My Friends

| Blue | Green | Brown |

X marks the "plot"!

◄ These sisters have blue eyes and brown eyes. What color are your friends' eyes?

A pictogram (also called a pictograph) is another way to show results. It uses pictures to show numbers of things. For example, if you want to draw a pictogram showing how many adult teeth your friends have it might look like this:

▼ Ask your friends to count their adult teeth, and then give you the results.

How Many Adult Teeth Do My Friends Have?

Eva

Sam

Tariq

LINE GRAPHS

Bar graphs, line plots, and pictograms are great for recording some kinds of data. But let's say you want to show the temperature in four different places around your home during the year. The places could be your basement, garage, and outside in the yard (in the sun and in the shade). You record the temperatures in each place on the first of each month.

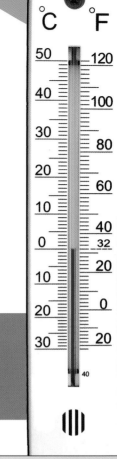

▶ You measure temperature with a thermometer, like this one.

Your table might look like this:

Date	Basement temperature		Garage temperature		Yard temperature (in sun)		Yard temperature (in shade)	
	°F	°C	°F	°C	°F	°C	°F	°C
January 1	39	4	37	2.75	28	-2.25	28	-2.25
February 1	39	4	37	2.75	30	-1	30	-1
March 1	41	5	41	5	48	9	46	7.75
April 1	43	6	50	10	59	15	54	12.25
May 1	45	7.25	59	15	66	19	61	16
June 1	46	7.75	68	20	84	29	77	25
July 1	46	7.75	72	22.25	91	32.75	81	27.25
August 1	46	7.75	75	24	91	32.75	81	27.25
September 1	46	7.75	68	20	81	27.25	68	20
October 1	45	7.25	59	15	68	20	61	16
November 1	43	6	50	10	55	12.75	48	9
December 1	39	4	39	4	32	0	32	0

It would be difficult to show these results in a bar graph, line plot, or pictogram. For these results a **line graph** will work best. To make a line graph in this example, draw a horizontal and a vertical line on graph paper (just like a bar graph). You write the temperature in Fahrenheit up the vertical line, and the dates along the horizontal line.

You must put in the data for one location at a time. Draw dots to show the different temperatures during each month of the year. Then, use a ruler to join the dots together to make a line. Now do the same for the next location. Make sure you draw each location in a different color. Your graph will look similar to this:

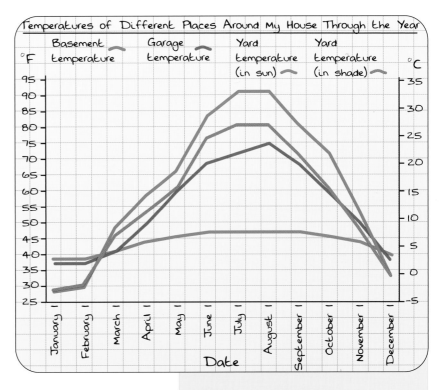

◀ This man is recording temperature and rainfall. He will then add the results to a climate graph.

Climate Graphs

The climate of a place is its weather over a long period of time. Climate is often displayed using graphs. The amount of rain that falls each month is usually shown as a bar graph. Temperatures are usually recorded as a line graph.

LET'S EXPERIMENT!

Color and Heat

Materials:
- ☑ two glasses of the same size
- ☑ one piece of white construction paper
- ☑ one piece of black construction paper
- ☑ scissors
- ☑ tap water
- ☑ tape
- ☑ a thermometer
- ☑ a pencil
- ☑ paper or journal
- ☑ graph paper
- ☑ a ruler

Problem
Have you ever touched the blacktop on your driveway on a sunny day? Have you noticed how warm it gets? Is it warmer than the concrete on the sidewalk? Which do you think heats up faster, a dark surface or a light-colored one? Make a hypothesis, then try this experiment!

1 Cover the outside of one glass in the white paper. Tape the paper in place. Cut a square out of the leftover white paper. Make sure it is big enough to cover the top of your glass.

2 Do the same with the other glass, but this time use the black paper.

3   Fill the glasses with the same amount of water. Make sure you don't get your paper wet.

4   Make a table for your data. With the thermometer, take the temperature of the water in both glasses. Leave the thermometer in for a minute before you read the temperature. Write down the temperature in your table.

5   Put both of your glasses in a sunny place, like a windowsill. Put the square of white paper on the glass covered in white paper. Put the square of black paper on the glass covered in black paper.

6   Take the temperature of both glasses every five minutes for an hour. Write down your results.

7   Draw a graph of your results on the graph paper. What do they show? Did you prove your hypothesis?

Think About it

What kind of graph do you think will be good to show your results? Remember, you will need to show the data for the two different glasses. You will want to compare the temperature of the water in the glass with white paper to the water in the glass with black paper. What kind of graph would help you do that?

FIGURING IT OUT

Drawing graphs is a great start, but it is not enough on its own. Scientists know that they have to figure out what those graphs are telling them. This is called *interpretation*, or "making an *inference*."

In our plant experiments, our graph on page 11 showed us that a fertilized plant grew at a certain speed, up to a certain height. The non-fertilized plant did not grow as quickly and did not get as tall, even though it started off at the same height as the fertilized plant. So, what does this graph tell us?

◄ The results of our plant experiment were simple to interpret. Sometimes interpreting data can take many months or years.

The graph tells us that the fertilizer we added did help the plant to grow. We can clearly see that the non-fertilized plant did not grow as quickly. We can conclude from this experiment that adding fertilizer to one of the plants once a week helped it grow three and a half inches (8.75 cm) taller than the plant without fertilizer over an eight-week period.

Nobel loved his work. He thought it was a blast!

Explosive Experiments!

In the middle of the 19th century, Alfred Nobel (below) tried many experiments to find a safe way of handling nitroglycerine. Nitroglycerine is a powerful explosive. Nobel's younger brother was killed in an explosion caused by the substance. Nobel had to be very careful to interpret the results of his experiments correctly! By accident, Nobel discovered that if nitroglycerine was mixed with a material such as clay it could be handled quite easily. This discovery helped Nobel invent dynamite.

INTERPRETING LINE GRAPHS

Line graphs, like the one on page 17, are great for plotting different measurements in different places and at different times. What can we interpret from our graph of temperatures taken at different places around the home?

First, we found out that the temperature in the basement does not change much at all. It stays cool down there even in the heat of summer, but the temperature does not drop much even in a cold winter. Why do you think this is?

▲ Your temperature readings will depend upon the climate where you live.

The temperature in the garage changes a lot more, but it still doesn't reach the freezing mark in winter. Outside in the shade, there is a big change of temperature through the year. But this change is not as big as the temperature change out in the sun.

In the Home

It would be a very different experiment if you took temperatures from rooms around the house. Why do you think this is? (Clue: think about any ways you and your family control the temperatures around your home. How might these affect your results?)

▲ What do you think will affect the temperature in this room?

INTERPRET THIS!

Sometimes, it is impossible to use a graph to show the results of an experiment. The results cannot be measured in terms of numbers. But it is still important to get those results in order and to interpret them. For example, imagine an experiment in which you wanted to see how leaf color changed in the fall.

◄ Leaves turn to many different colors in the fall.

It would be hard to graph what happened, but you could organize the results in a chart like this:

Week	Leaf color
week 1	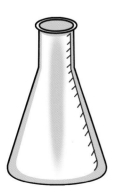
week 2	
week 3	
week 4	

We can interpret this chart to see that, over 28 days, the leaf color changed from green, to pale green, to orange, to brown.

People Watching

Some scientists study human behavior. They often base their interpretations and conclusions mostly on observations, not numbers. Margaret Mead (below) studied a group of people living on the islands of Samoa in the 1920s. Most of her data was in the form of written observations. She couldn't make graphs of this sort of data, but she did make some useful interpretations. She concluded that the Samoans grew from being children to adults without many of the problems that children faced in the United States.

WHAT'S NEXT?

Now you have covered this step of the scientific method! You know that it is important to organize your data in ways that are easy to understand. This helps you to clearly see what happened in your experiment. Then, you can begin interpreting the results. Now, you are ready for the last step of the scientific method.

Remember that in Step 2, you made a hypothesis. This was an "educated guess" about what your experiment would prove. Using the graphs and interpretations you have made in Step 5, you can now see if the hypothesis was correct.

The Tide Turns

One of history's great scientists, Galileo Galilei, made many great hypotheses. One he got wrong was his idea about how **tides** work in large areas of water. But the "guesswork" Galilei did on tides helped many later scientists find out how tides really work. Now we know tides are caused by the moon.

Galilei's hypothesis didn't hold water but it helped other scientists discover the truth.

▲ You might want to share the results of your experiments with your friends or your teacher.

Then you can make some conclusions about your experiment.

Once you have made your conclusions, what comes next? Scientists share their conclusions with other people.

You can share your conclusions with your friends. You might want to present your experiment and conclusions at a science fair at school.

Good luck!

KEEPING A JOURNAL

Do you like to travel? Do you take photographs when you go on vacation? Photographs are a great way to remember what the places you have visited looked like. But what if you wanted to record other things you enjoyed, like the sounds, tastes, and smells?

The best way to do this would be to make a travel journal. You could write down everywhere you've been, and how it felt to be there. You could also add photographs and maps to your journal.

Scientists work the same way. They keep records of every stage of an experiment. That way they can check back to see what they did, and when they did it.

A journal really helps if something doesn't look right in your experiment. Let's say in our plant experiment on pages 6-7 you suddenly found that the plant without fertilizer seemed to be doing better than the plant with fertilizer. You might check back in your journal and find that you made a mistake. Halfway through the project, you mixed up Plants 1 and 2 and fed the wrong one the fertilizer! Without a journal, you would not know what had happened.

◄ Make sure you draw your graphs in your journal neatly and carefully.

Here are some tips for keeping your journal:

• Think carefully about what kind of graph is best for the data you have;

• When drawing your graph, always check back to your table to make sure you've got everything right;

• Don't interpret your data just to fit the hypothesis you made earlier! If the data shows something else, it means your conclusion will be different than your hypothesis. But that is still good science.

Stay on the "write" track. Keep a journal!

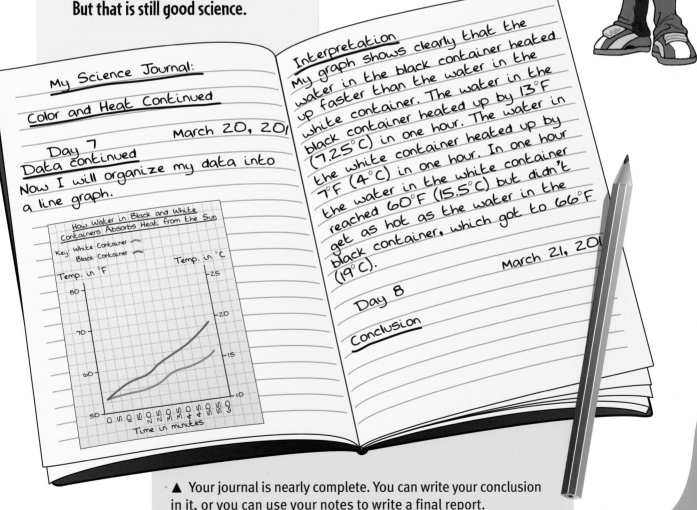

My Science Journal:

Color and Heat Continued

Day 7   March 20, 201

Data continued

Now I will organize my data into a line graph.

How Water in Black and White Containers Absorbs Heat from the Sun

Key: White Container ~
     Black Container ~

Temp. in °F   Temp. in °C

80   —25

70   —20

                          —15

60

                          —10

50
   0 5 10 15 20 25 30 35 40 45 50 55 60
        Time in minutes

Interpretation

My graph shows clearly that the water in the black container heated up faster than the water in the white container. The water in the black container heated up by 13°F (7.25°C) in one hour. The water in the white container heated up by 7°F (4°C) in one hour. In one hour the water in the white container reached 60°F (15.5°C) but didn't get as hot as the water in the black container, which got to 66°F (19°C).

                    March 21, 201

Day 8

Conclusion

▲ Your journal is nearly complete. You can write your conclusion in it, or you can use your notes to write a final report.

29

TIMELINE

Below is a list of important discoveries—and the people who organized the results.

Year	Discovery or invention	Who interpreted the data?
240BC	Earth's circumference measured	Eratosthenes observes the difference in the location of the sun in the sky in different parts of Egypt on the summer solstice. By interpreting his data he can estimate how big Earth is around the equator.
1687	How the tides work	For centuries data shows that the cycle of the moon affects the tides. However, it isn't until Isaac Newton publishes his important conclusions about gravity that it becomes clear *why* the moon has an effect.
1786	The first graphs	William Playfair uses bar graphs and line graphs for the first time in his book *The Commercial and Political Atlas*.
1854	London cholera outbreak	Careful data analysis shows Dr. John Snow that all the **cholera** sufferers in a part of London have been drinking from the same water pump. The pump is taken out of use and the outbreak ends.
1920s	*Coming of Age in Samoa*	Margaret Mead draws many important conclusions from her written data about what it is like to be a girl growing up in Samoa. She publishes a book called *Coming of Age in Samoa*.
2009	Spreading universe	From data sent by the Hubble Space Telescope, scientists are able to interpret how fast the universe is spreading out. Their interpretation is more accurate than any previous ones.

GLOSSARY

anomaly Something that is unusual or unexpected

bar graph A graph that uses colored bars to show the results of an experiment

chart A way of showing numbers in rows and columns. It is also called a table

cholera A serious disease that can spread through drinking water

data Scientific information

diagram A neat and detailed picture showing how things fit together or how a system works. Diagrams have a title and labels

graph A diagram that can illustrate the results of an experiment. A graph has one measurement along the bottom, and another up the side

horizontal Describes something that is lying flat, like a line across a page

hypothesis An educated guess about what an experiment will prove

imperial A system of measurement used in some countries, like the United States. It includes inches, pounds, and degrees Fahrenheit

inference Making a conclusion from data

interpretation Looking at data and thinking about what it shows

journal A record of every step of an experiment

line graph A graph that uses lines and measurements to show the results of an experiment

metric A system of measurement used by most scientists. It includes centimeters, grams, and degrees Celsius

observation Noticing something happening by using the five senses

research Finding out facts about something

results The information that comes from an experiment

scientific method The way to do an experiment properly

table A way of showing numbers in rows and columns. Also called a chart

tally chart A chart or table on which you make marks and then add them together to make a number

tide The daily rising and falling of the sea

trend The pattern of how things change over time

vertical Describes something that is upright, like a line that goes up and down a page

FURTHER INFORMATION

Books

Science in Seconds for Kids: Over 100 Experiments You Can Do in Ten Minutes or Less, Jean Potter, Jossey-Bass, January 1995

Janice VanCleave's Big Book of Play and Find Out Science Projects, Janice VanCleave, Jossey-Bass, March 2007

Web sites

coolcosmos.ipac.caltech.edu *and go to the "Cosmic Kids" section.*

www.bbc.co.uk/schools/podsmission/

INDEX